performed by **Neil Sedaka**   illustrated by **Tim Bowers**

DINOSAUR PET

children's lyrics by **Marc Sedaka**

inspired by "Calendar Girl" by
Neil Sedaka & Howard Greenfield

imagine!
Publishing

I love, I love, I love
my dinosaur pet.
Yeah, sweet dinosaur pet.

I love, I love, I love
my dinosaur pet.
Each and every day of the year.

January,
he's **breaking out**
of his shell.

February,

his body's starting to swell.

March,

at least **eight times a day**
he's got to be fed.

April,

when he sleeps with me he
crushes the bed.

Yeah, yeah, how big
can he get?

I love, I love, I love
my little dinosaur pet.

Every day, every day, every day,
every day of the year,
Every day of the year.

May,

maybe if the roof was **twice as tall.**

June,

he wouldn't bump it when
he's roaming the hall.

July,
like the fireworks,
he touches the sky.

August,

the cost of groceries is
bleeding us dry.

Yeah, yeah, how big
can he get?

I love, I love, I love
my little dinosaur pet.

Every day, every day, every day,
every day of the year,
Every day of the year.

Yeah, yeah, how big
can he get?

I love, I love, I love
my little dinosaur pet.

Every day, every day, every day,
every day of the year,
Every day of the year.

September,

just the tail alone is
thirty feet long.

October,

when we **trick or treat**
he goes as **King Kong.**

November,
fifty turkeys
weren't nearly enough.

Yeah, yeah, how big
can he get?

I love, I love, I love
my little dinosaur pet.

December,
come the new year things are **gonna get rough.**

Every day, every day, every day,
every day of the year,
Every day of the year.

I love, I love, I love
my dinosaur pet.
Yeah, sweet dinosaur pet.

I love, I love, I love
my dinosaur pet.
Yeah, sweet dinosaur pet.

I love, I love, I love
my dinosaur pet.
Yeah, sweet dinosaur pet.

I love, I love, I love
my dinosaur pet.

Performer's Note

This is our second children's book in hopefully a series of many. On this book, I collaborated with my son Marc Sedaka, who wrote the new lyric to the original tune of "Calendar Girl," my hit record from 1961. My five-year-old grandson Michael is a dinosaur fanatic, and it was he who inspired the book. I hope you also enjoy the three-song CD, which includes "Dinosaur Pet" and two brand-new Neil Sedaka songs: "She Moved Away" and "The Tooth Fairy." I am delighted that I am now reaching the young generation of book readers, after the success of *Waking Up Is Hard to Do*. Please enjoy the story and the songs.

Illustrator's Note

Songs can remind us of people and places throughout our lives. Neil Sedaka's songs are attached to many fond memories from my earlier years, growing up in Ohio. Now, a new generation will build memories together with familiar songs to mark those special times, and once again, Neil Sedaka's songs will help mark memories. I'm so glad to be able to contribute the artwork that will accompany his wonderful music. With the recent arrival of our first grandchild, my wife and I look forward to sharing a chorus of "I love, I love, I love my dinosaur pet" and the great memories it will create for years to come.

Library of Congress Cataloging-in-Publication Data

Sedaka, Marc.
Dinosaur pet / children's lyrics by Marc Sedaka ;
performed by Neil Sedaka; illustrated by Tim Bowers.
p. cm.
"Inspired by Calendar Girl by Neil Sedaka
and Howard Greenfield." Performer, Neil Sedaka.

Summary: Provides new lyrics to the tune of Sedaka's
song, Calendar Girl, in which a dinosaur hatches in
January, then grows bigger every month of the year.
Accompanying CD has a performance of the title song
as well as two original songs.

ISBN 978-1-936140-36-7 (hardcover)
1. Songs, English--United States--Texts. [1. Songs.]
I. Sedaka, Neil. II. Bowers, Tim, ill. III. Greenfield, Howard.
IV. Title. PZ8.3.S44428Din 2012 782.42--dc23 [E]
2011025358
10 9 8 7 6 5 4 3 2

An Imagine Book
Published by Charlesbridge
85 Main Street
Watertown, MA 02472
617-926-0329
www.charlesbridge.com

Children's Lyrics by Marc Sedaka
Illustrated by Tim Bowers
Inspired by "Calendar Girl" by Howard Greenfield
and Neil Sedaka
Performed by Neil Sedaka

US Copyright
"Dinosaur Pet" By Neil Sedaka and Howard Greenfield;
children's lyrics by Marc Sedaka
© 2009 Neil Sedaka Music, Master Courtesy of Razor & Tie
Direct, LLC. "Calendar Girl" written by Howard Greenfield
and Neil Sedaka © 1961 SCREEN GEMS-EMI MUSIC INC.
Copyright renewed 1989 SCREEN GEMS-EMI MUSIC INC./
CAREERS-BMG MUSIC INC. All Rights Reserved. International
Copyright Secured. Used by permission.

World copyright exclusive of the US
"Dinosaur Pet" By Neil Sedaka and Howard Greenfield;
children's lyrics by Marc Sedaka
© 2009 Neil Sedaka Music, Master Courtesy of Razor & Tie
Direct, LLC. "Calendar Girl" written by Howard Greenfield
and Neil Sedaka © 1961 Renewed 1989 SCREEN GEMS-EMI
MUSIC INC. All Rights Reserved. International Copyright
Secured. Used by permission.

Illustrations copyright © 2012 by Tim Bowers

CD Copyrights and Details

"Dinosaur Pet"
By Howard Greenfield and Neil Sedaka
Children's Lyrics by Marc Sedaka
Performed by Neil Sedaka
© 2009 Neil Sedaka Music, Master Courtesy of Razor
& Tie Direct, LLC. Universal Music–Careers and EMI Music
Publishing. All Rights Reserved.

"The Tooth Fairy"
Words and Music by Neil Sedaka
Performed by Neil Sedaka
© 2009 Neil Sedaka Music
All Rights Reserved.
International Copyright Secured
Used by permission.

"She Moved Away"
Words and Music by Neil Sedaka
Performed by Neil Sedaka
© 2009 Neil Sedaka Music
All Rights Reserved.
International Copyright Secured
Used by permission.

Printed in China

Manufactured in June 2012
All rights reserved, including the right of reproduction
in whole or in part in any form. Charlesbridge
and colophon are registered trademarks of
Charlesbridge Publishing, Inc.
ISBN 13: 978-1-936140-36-7

For information about custom editions, special sales,
premium and corporate purchases, please contact
Charlesbridge Publishing, Inc.
at specialsales@charlesbridge.com

For my grandchildren Charlotte,
Amanda, and Michael. –NS

To my grandson, Caleb. –TB